Henry Explores the Mountains

MARK TAYLOR

Illustrations by

GRAHAM BOOTH

Atheneum 1975 *New York*

LIBRARY OF CONGRESS CATALOGING IN PUBLICATION DATA

Taylor, Mark.
Henry explores the mountains.
SUMMARY: Henry's outing in the woods with his dog
involves him in a forest fire, heroism, and
a helicopter ride.
[1. Forest fires—Fiction]   I. Booth, Graham, illus.
II. Title.   PZ7.T2172Hdc   [E]   74-19315
ISBN 0-689-30461-7

Published simultaneously in Canada by
McClelland & Stewart Ltd.
Manufactured in the United States of America
Printed by Connecticut Printers, Inc., Hartford

First Edition

On the night of the big frost, Henry and Laird Angus McAngus looked at Henry's posters of mountains.

"Angus," said Henry, "we had better explore the mountains before winter sets in."

Angus thumped his tail excitedly.

"Tomorrow will be the day," said Henry.

The next morning before breakfast, Henry made ready
his explorer's kit. He filled it extra full of flags.
Then he asked his father for some long rope.

"Why do you need rope?" asked his father.

"We're heading into the wild and untracked mountains,"
said Henry. "You always need rope when climbing in
the mountains—for safety."

"And why are you taking so many flags?" asked his
father.

"I expect to make a new trail," replied Henry.
"Angus and I will be trailblazers."

While he ate breakfast, Henry told his mother and father all about exploring mountains.

"In which direction do the untracked mountains lie?" asked Henry's mother.

"North," said Henry. "The trip will be long and hard."

"Well, please be very careful," said his mother, as she packed an extra big lunch.

"Explorers are always careful," said Henry, "because they never know what to expect."

"I expect you to be home before dark," said Henry's father.

"Of course," said Henry.

It was a bright autumn morning
as they started out.

"Angus," said Henry, "I wonder what
we will find in those wild mountains."

After a long trek, Henry and Angus came to some hills.

"These are called foothills," Henry explained. "First you come to the foothills, and then you come to the mountains."

Henry looked back at the trail of flags. "I think we are blazing a good trail," he said proudly.

When Henry and Augus came to a valley, they saw herds
of wild game. Then Angus spotted a deer and chased it.

Henry ran after them. Angus barked and barked.

"Keep a steady head, Angus!" called Henry.

By the time Angus stopped chasing the deer, they were in a place where there were steep cliffs.

"We are now in the mountains, and this is a mountain canyon," said Henry. "We must be careful to stick together. We must avoid falling or getting caught in an avalanche."

Avalanche was Henry's favorite new word.

"And we must be on the lookout for bears and wolves," warned Henry.

When Angus spied a fox, he started to chase it.

"Watch out!" cried Henry.

Angus slipped off the edge of the canyon.
But the rope kept him from falling too far.

"You were almost a goner," said Henry. "Now you see why mountain climbers and explorers need good strong rope."

Then Henry said, "We'll call this Angus Canyon."

It was dark and lonely in the mountains. Henry was surprised
when they met a wolf. There was hardly time to think. But
Angus was very brave and barked as hard as he could.

Just in time an old man appeared.

"This is my dog, and I call him Wolf," he explained. "He is old and toothless, but he is a good watchdog."

"Well, I'm an explorer," said Henry. "I'm pretty used to surprises. This is my dog, and I call him Laird Angus McAngus."

Henry and Angus came to the top of the mountains at last. "This will be Mount Henry forever," Henry declared. And he claimed it with his biggest flag.

Then Henry and Angus ate their lunch. Exploring mountains had made them very hungry.

Suddenly Angus ran over to the edge of the mountain and began to bark.

"What is the matter?" cried Henry.

When Henry looked over the edge, he saw what Angus was barking about. It was a forest fire!

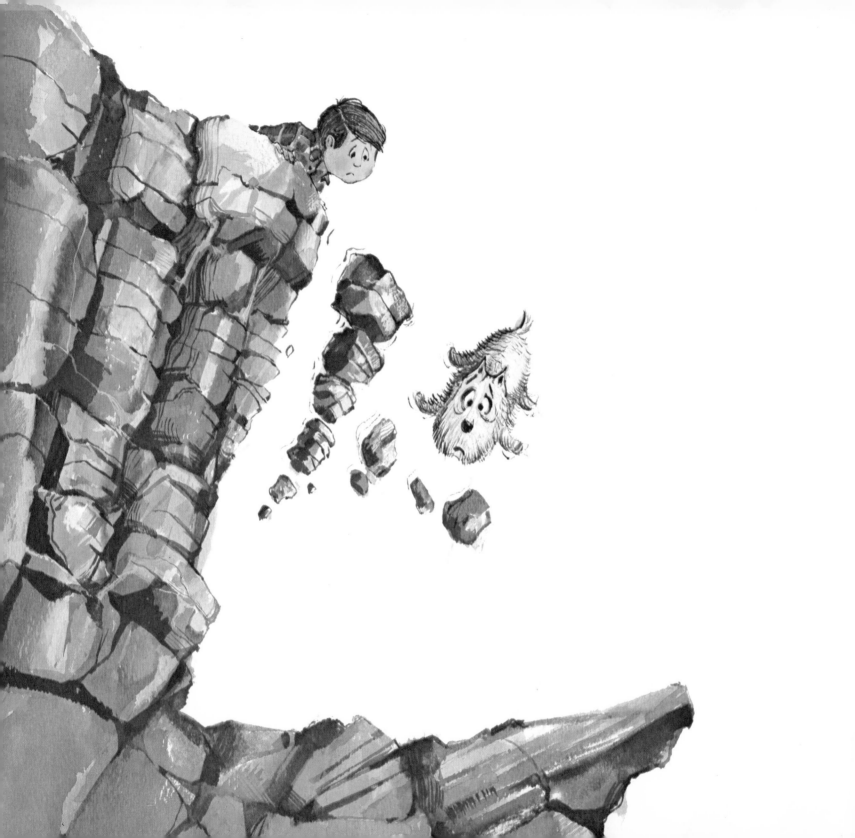

Angus was so excited he forgot to be careful. Suddenly there was an avalanche, and Angus was carried away! Henry narrowly escaped going with him.

When the avalanche was over, Henry tried to see what had happened to Angus.

Angus was out of reach. He lay very still. His eyes were closed.

"Angus! Angus!" shouted Henry.

But Angus did not move. And Henry could not get down to him.

"Grab the rope, Angus," Henry called. "I'll pull you up."

But Angus lay very still.

Below Angus was the fire. It was getting worse.

Henry was in a terrible predicament. There was only one thing to do—find help.

Henry ran as fast as he could. Luckily he had his
trail of flags to follow.

Henry ran to the old man's cabin and told him about Angus and about the fire.

The old man telephoned for help.

"We must hurry," said Henry.

Things happened fast. A helicopter landed right
on top of Mount Henry. And down below a fire truck
came to fight the forest fire.

Henry and the old man told the pilot what had
happened. The pilot was a forest ranger.

"When I saw a trail of flags below, I knew which
way to fly," said the ranger. "Those flags made
a good trail for me."

Another ranger came, and he was very brave. Quickly he went to rescue Angus. It was a dangerous task.

Henry and the old man did all they could to help.

Angus was all right. He had just had his breath knocked out.
Everybody praised him for discovering the fire in time.

Then Henry and Angus got a ride home in the helicopter. It
was very exciting.

The ranger followed Henry's trail. Henry explained how
flags are useful to explorers.

Henry's mother and father were amazed to see
Henry and Angus in a helicopter.

"What happened?" they both asked at once.

"We helped put out a forest fire," said Henry.

"One never knows what to expect from this
explorer," said Henry's mother.

"That's right," Henry agreed.

Henry and the ranger explained everything that
had happened.

"Henry and Angus are heroes," said the ranger.

"It was the most exciting day of my life," said Henry.
"And everything came out all right . . ."

". . . thanks to my flags."